RUNT
FARM

THE
GARDEN

Runt Farm

Under New Management

Amanda Lorenzo

Illustrations by

Mark Evan Walker

Bookti Mookti PRESS

SEATTLE, WASHINGTON

Contents

~No time for that now, Junior. Best be movin' on.

Cracking Up in the Barn

The old truck rattled and sputtered into the distance. Kitten crept out from his favorite hiding place in the old barn. He looked around quite satisfied with himself.

Cool, now I'm in charge! he thought. Of course there was very little left to be in charge of now, but Kitten hardly took notice.

Kitten nosed around in the piles of junk left behind by the Brunts. "Nice enough people, but we just didn't see eye to eye. Gonna miss that bowl of cream in the evenings, for sure. But

I never could bring myself to eat up little mice the way they wanted me to. 'Live and let live.' That's what I always say." He sharpened his claws on an old wicker chair, then headed out toward the pond for a kingly stroll.

Kitten had seen the pond many times, but today it looked better because it was all his. "I'm gonna call you Puddlefoot Pond," he said.

Kitten climbed the nearby hill. "Your name will be Picnic Hill," he said to the grass and the oak tree at the top. He circled the tree once and picked a spot to sit and watch the sun go down. "My first day as a farmer! Not bad."

Kitten had plans to see the stars come out, but a cold wind began to blow and he saw clouds making their way over the treetops toward the east. "*Brrr!*" he shivered. On any other evening Mrs. Brunt would be out by the barn calling, "Here, kitty-kitty-kitty!" Kitten listened. Nothing but the wind. "Time to go in, I guess," he said as he started back down the hill.

Kitten reached the barn just as the first raindrops began to fall. He climbed back up to his favorite place. He snuggled into his tattered black blanket and listened to the wind blow. *This is fun*, he thought. Night came. The barn creaked in the wind. Rain hammered against the roof. Kitten wished the moon would come out, but the clouds had pushed out the light. He heard a splash out by Puddlefoot Pond.

"Weasels?" Kitten wondered. He burrowed deeper into his blanket. "That's silly. Just go to sleep," he told himself, and after a while he dozed off.

The next morning as sunlight came poking through the cracks in the boards, Kitten heard something stirring.

Way up in the hay loft, a lone egg began to rock. Then it began to roll. The egg began to shake and, yes, rattle! Then with a hiccup it bounced over the side of the nesting box. The egg landed smack on the tummy of the sleepy cat.

"*Yaaahh!*" said
Kitten. "What's *that*?"

Not a sound from the
egg. Kitten sniffed at it. A
crack appeared on one side.
The egg made a quick hop. Kitten
leaped, arched his back, and hissed, "It's alive!"
Another little hiccup, and the egg began
bouncing every which way.

Kitten crouched and circled the egg. Cracks
began showing all over it. Kitten put his ear up
close. He heard a tiny *click, click, click!*

Whatever's in there, it sure wants out, he thought.

Something hard poked through the biggest
crack. "Peep," said the egg. "Peep, peep, peep."

"Hey, you're a duck!" said Kitten. "Anybody
can see that by the shape of your bill. What's

your name, duck?"

"Peep," said the egg.

"Well okay, then! Good enough!" said Kitten.

Just then The Peep gave a tremendous push and popped all the way out of the egg. "Peep, peep, peep!" Kitten was pretty sure that meant The Peep was happy to be free.

"You can call me Kitten," said the cat.

"Peeeeep," said The Peep. Kitten decided that meant, "Okay."

"You got some shell on your head there, Peep. Kinda cool though, uh . . . like a hat." He didn't want to offend the little guy.

"Peep, peep, peep," the duck piped.

What did it mean? It could have meant, "Mind your own business, Nosey!" or "Glad you like it—my own design, you know," or maybe, "*Aaah* . . . get this thing off my head!"

Kitten thought he knew what it meant,
but something told him to keep his paws off.
"Look, it will come off on its own. Don't worry
little guy," he said. At that The Peep heaved a
big sigh, and sure enough the shell plopped off
his head.

It was like that all day long. Whenever he
heard *Peep, peep, peep!* Kitten seemed to know
exactly what The Peep meant to say.

Peep, peep, peep meant "I'm hungry. When
do we eat?"

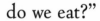

Peep, peep, peep also meant
"I'm sleepy. Where's my
nesting box?"

Sometimes *Peep, peep,
peep* meant "Can we go
swimming?"

Kitten hated swimming, but he showed his

new friend out to Puddlefoot Pond anyway. Kitten watched as The Peep paddled around. *Man, he swims pretty good for a guy who's only one day old,* he thought.

At the end of the day, The Peep stood next to Kitten and nuzzled his fur. "Peep, peep, peep," he said. And this time it meant "I love you."

"Aw, dude!" Kitten chuckled. "You're a doofy little guy, aren't ya?"

Before long it grew dark. The Peep fluffed up and settled in. Soon Kitten heard soft snoring sounds. *Peeep, peeep, peeep.* It meant "I want to stay with you forever!" And even though for one good, long day Kitten had done all right on his own, he liked the sound of that.

A Basket Is Born

Kitten woke up early the next day and stretched like a Halloween cat. The barn seemed awfully quiet. Kitten leaped down from the stack of hay bales. Maybe The Peep was exploring the barn. "Nope," said Kitten.

He wandered outside and searched every row of the weedy kitchen garden.

"Now where could that little fella be?" said Kitten, a little worried.

Then Kitten saw something moving out on

Puddlefoot Pond. Sure enough, The Peep was swimming in big circles, flapping and splashing and peeping away. Kitten watched as The Peep swam right into the tall reeds at the edge of the pond.

Suddenly The Peep burst out of the reeds into the middle of the pond. As he swam, he blurted a string of excited chatter. "Peep, peep, peep! . . . Peep, peep, peep!" Paddling furiously, The Peep did figure eights over the rippling surface of the pond. Kitten sidled up next to the bunch of reeds to get a better look. He was amazed that such a little duck could cover so much surface area in so little time.

"What's he doin' out there?" Kitten wondered.

Kitten watched as The Peep swam back and forth, first out into the middle of the pond,

then back deep into the dark green reed bed.
The reeds shook and swayed. Each time The
Peep swam into sight, he was even more excited,
splashing and peeping and making fresh
patterns in the water. Then back into the dense
clump of reeds he went. Now and then a few
bits of green flew up into the air.

Kitten wished like crazy he could see what
The Peep was doing! He nosed and pawed his
way into the thicket trying to get closer, but it
was wet and mushy in there so he backed out.

Suddenly The Peep emerged from the reed bed pushing a strange-looking object.

"Peep, peep," he said. He sounded a little out of breath.

"For me?" Kitten asked.

"Peep, peeeeeep!" exclaimed the little duck.

"You can say that again!" said Kitten. "Artistic, too," he added.

"Peep, peep?"

"Well, sure it's a basket! I can see that by all this curvy weaving. You bet," said Kitten.

"'Reed Basket, by The Peep.' This oughta be in a museum, dude. Thanks."

Kitten batted the rim of the Reed Basket with his paw, and it tipped over on top of him. With a playful *"Yeeow!"* and a leap, Kitten ran off. The Peep hurried after him, squawking and flapping. The two ran through the kitchen garden, around the barn, and all the way back to the edge of the pond.

As they reached the water's edge, The Peep ran up and butted the Reed Basket. It flipped again! Kitten and The Peep flipped too, and they both ended up inside. "Peep, peep!" The Peep squeaked with delight. The force of the collision sent the Reed Basket out onto the waters of Puddlefoot Pond.

"Dude! Hey!" Kitten looked about wildly for a dry way out of the basket. There wasn't any.

"I'm a cat, not a water lily," Kitten complained.

"Peep, peep, peep." The Peep leaned happily over the side. He blew bubbles in the water. The Reed Basket tipped and bobbed. Kitten clung to the side, watching as they moved farther and farther from dry land. The Peep's bubble-blowing pushed their basket boat out into the middle of the pond.

"Stop that!" cried Kitten. "Too far, man!"

"Peep, peep," said The Peep, meaning "Please forgive me. It's only water. I love water! I thought you would, too."

"I hear you, buddy, but just blow over here on this side, okay? Back to dry land now . . . " Kitten didn't take his eyes off the pond's edge.

He could hardly wait to feel his paws on
dry ground.

Before long the Reed Basket bumped up
onto the shore, and Kitten made a quick leap
to safety.

"Peep, peep, peep," said The Peep.

"Yeah, that is some Reed Basket, all right.
We'll have fun with that, for sure. Just not feet-
wettin' fun, okay?"

"Peep, peep," said The Peep, quick to agree.

"Hey, what if this thing had wheels? Hop
in, dude. We'll take her for a spin!" Kitten and
The Peep pretended they were
driving all the way around
Puddlefoot Pond. The Peep
pretended it was as much
fun as basket boating.

"Peep, peep, peep?"

"Sure, it can be a pup tent," said Kitten. They stopped and rolled the Reed Basket over on top of them. It was dark and cozy. The Peep nuzzled Kitten, who yawned.

"Let's take it back to the barn now. I need a nap!" said Kitten. They tipped the basket on its side and rolled it back toward the barn. Back and forth they wibbled and wobbled the Reed Basket. At last they plunked it down in a circle of sunlight near the hay bales. Kitten yawned. "Perfect, man. This is just the place for a snooze."

"Peeeeep, peep, peep," said the yellow duckling.

"I had fun too, buddy," Kitten said, closing his eyes and curling up in the Reed Basket.

"Peep."

Kitten didn't mind The Peep wanting to

have the last word. The little duck climbed in next to Kitten and was the first to fall asleep. After a few minutes The Peep began making those little snoring sounds. But Kitten didn't mind that, either. In fact, he kind of liked it.

Neither cat nor duck knew just how exciting life was about to become.

Cletus and Tooth Drop In

Far from Runt Farm, two mice hurried through the woods. All their lives they had lived at NAARF, the Nightshade Association Animal Research Facility. But on this day they had seized the opportunity to escape. Up and down they ran, over hillocks, through clumps of wild irises, past stumps and bushes, for what seemed an eternity. And yet they could still see the ominous building behind them.

"Dear me, Cletus, we've come so far and

my feet are quite sore," sighed the female as she slowed to a walk. "How will we know when we've come far enough?"

"Well, Tooth, I'm not sure even Grandma Nellie would know how far away is far enough," her friend replied.

"Grandma Nellie . . . how I miss her," said Tooth. "She was the very first of us to be made extra-smart by that nefarious bunch at NAARF. But now she's gone, the dear soul. There never will be another mouse like her."

GRANDMA NELLIE

"Yes, and I'm fairly certain we wouldn't have lasted much longer. I can only think that they will search everywhere for us. We are unique among mice, my dear," Cletus said.

"Oh, I'm sure they are feeling the loss of a

pair that reads, invents, cooks, and doctors, but they must never find us," Tooth said, picking up the pace. "We must avoid that place at all costs!"

"Yes, indeed," said Cletus, "the life of a NAARF mouse is a mixed blessing. Engaged in fascinating research . . . but prisoners. I'll miss the cheese, to be sure . . . and I had hoped to finish my improvements to the electron microscope . . . " His voice trailed off.

"Well, I for one will not miss a thing about that awful place," said Tooth, "but I do feel terrible leaving cousin Clovis behind."

"If only she weren't so darned comfortable in that penthouse cage," said Cletus, shaking his head. He caught sight of an

COUSIN CLOVIS

inviting puddle and headed for it.

"I hope they allow her to go on painting," Tooth continued. "She'd be lost without her art."

"Well, worry won't help, my dear. Let's just rest our feet in this cool mud and think for a bit." Cletus stopped, and plopping down beside the puddle he dangled his feet in. *"Aahh."* He began stroking his whiskers thoughtfully.

Tooth suddenly froze. "Cletus, what is that? I hear something."

Suddenly a weasel came splashing toward them, teeth bared and ready to bite.

"Tooth! Get back! Quick!" Cletus stepped  up and brandished his cane like a sword to challenge the weasel.

"Oh, no you don't!" hissed Cletus. "We haven't come this far to be eaten by you!"

"May as well be eaten by me," the weasel snarled. "How long can you last out here? I've seen you NAARF types before. Coddled and cage-fed. Easy pickin's for me and m'pals." He opened his mouth and snapped the cane in half with one bite.

"I warn you, sir, we are not ordinary mice! Back off now, or you'll be sorry!" Cletus commanded, standing his ground.

"Cletus, we must run!" Tooth fretted. The weasels she had known at NAARF were fearsome, every one. What's more, they stank.

"Yes, you should run, missy." The weasel grinned, showing his sharp teeth. "More fun for me." He moved so near they could feel the heat of his bad breath. It smelled of . . . Tooth couldn't bear to identify the stench.

"You're the one who should be running!" cried Cletus. He stuck out his right leg and wiggled it directly under the weasel's nose.

"Hah!" said the weasel, biting down hard. "*Yeeowww!* You broke my tooth, you . . . What are you, a mouse or a machine?" the weasel howled.

"I warned you!" shouted Cletus. "We are the most dangerous kind of mice. Remember that, and tell all your friends!"

The weasel bounded off over the hill,

whimpering loudly.

"Cletus," said Tooth, "that was a most impressive example of self-defense! How did you do it?"

"Why, that old scalawag bit down on my titanium leg brace, dear. See?" Cletus raised his

pant leg as a reminder. The clunky NAARF-made brace had often bothered Cletus, but now

. . . well, he saw it had possibilities.

"And now a certain weasel believes you and I are made of titanium through and through!" Cletus chuckled.

"That's right, your brace! How serendipitous!" said Tooth.

"Yes, good fortune is on our side for now," said Cletus. "It's best we keep going . . . in case that wag of a weasel comes back to check the composition of my other leg."

The two came over a rise near an enormous oak tree. From there they could see a barn with a small pond nearby. "What a beautiful little farm. Do you think anyone lives there?" asked Tooth. "And if so, are they the sort who welcome visitors dropping in?"

"Nothing for it but to go and find out," said Cletus.

Tooth and Cletus started down the hill.
Forgetting it was broken, Cletus leaned on his
cane to steady himself. He lost his balance and
went tumbling!

"Oh my! Cletus!" cried
Tooth, running after him. But
her wish to help ran faster than
her legs could go. Tooth flew
head over
heels after her friend. At the
bottom of their tumble, the
two mice bumped right into
a basket.

"*Uuumph,*" groaned Cletus.

"*Oohh,*" said Tooth, rubbing
her side.

Tooth hurried to adjust her
spectacles. Cletus dusted off

his coat.

"Who would leave such a lovely basket out here in the weather, I wonder?" Tooth said.

"I would!" cried Kitten, leaping out to surprise them.

"Oh!" cried Tooth. She knew a cat when she saw one.

"Peep!" said The Peep.

"Dear me, Cletus," said Tooth. "It's a you-know-what! I hope he doesn't like titanium!"

"See here, cat," Cletus said, "we are . . .
very dangerous mice. I warn you against any
violence to our persons!"

"And we don't taste good at all," Tooth
added.

"We wouldn't eat you," Kitten said. "We
only eat stuff in jars, don't we, buddy?"

"Peep, peep!" agreed The Peep.

"He's just toying with us, Cletus. I suggest
you keep your cane and your leg . . . at the ready."

Kitten said, "My friend The Peep says,
'Please don't hurt us, dangerous mice. We want
to be friends, no kidding.'"

Tooth glanced at Cletus and smiled. The
cat and his little sidekick did seem genuinely
interested in friendship.

"Well, if that's the case then, my name is
Cletus. This is Tooth."

"I'm Kitten, and this is my place. And this is The Peep. He just hatched out."

"Yes, so it seems," said Tooth. "Nice to meet you both."

The Peep stepped forward. "Peep!" he said.

Cletus shook The Peep's wing. "I thought ducks said *quack*."

"Well, The Peep just said *peep* right from the git-go—never said *quack*—but I'm okay with it," said Kitten.

"Peep, peep! Peep, peep, peep!" The Peep hopped about.

Kitten said, "The Peep wants to know, do you want to play in the reed basket?"

"Dear me, I'm much too tired for that just now," said Tooth. "We've come a long way. Is there somewhere we might have a bit of a rest?"

"I know just the place. Over there's our

barn. You can stay as long as you want," said Kitten.

The Peep hopped into the basket, and Kitten hoisted it onto his head. The two led the way past the kitchen garden. Left untended, the rows were choked with weeds. Along the way, The Peep and Kitten pointed out all the best places to play. When they reached the barn, Tooth stopped.

"Look Cletus, this place is called Runt Farm."

Cletus looked around. "Seems like a normal-sized farm to me," he said.

"Well now, I believe it's rather a reference to animals who are smaller than their litter mates," said Tooth.

"Oh yes, of course. Well, it's as good a name as any, I suppose," said Cletus.

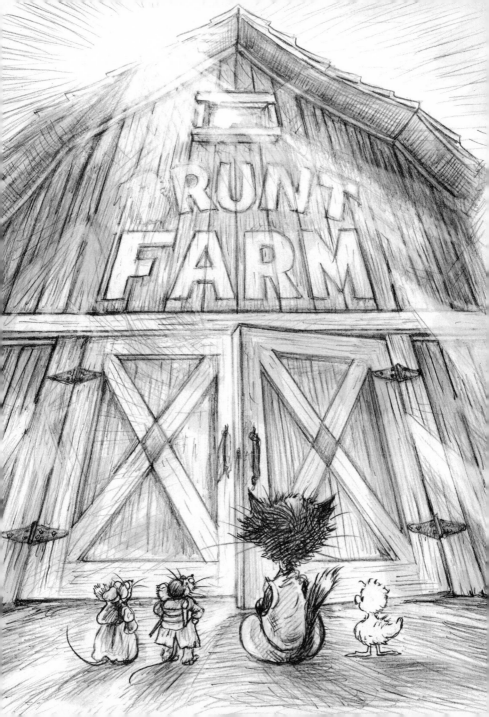

The group stepped into the musty barn. Cletus was delighted by what he saw! Piles of junk adorned three corners.

"Now, here you have endless possibilities," he said. "You know, I could make that reed basket of yours into a fine automobile, using a bit of this and that . . ."

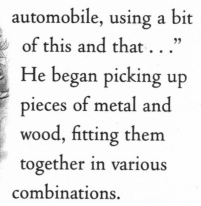

He began picking up pieces of metal and wood, fitting them together in various combinations.

"You could?" said Kitten. "Hey, that'd be great, man!" *Cool mice*, he thought.

"Peep, peep!" The Peep agreed, hopping right to left and left to right.

Stacked against the other side of the barn,

Tooth found boxes of clear glass bottles and tin cans.

"Look, Cletus—the perfect place for a kitchen. Hmm. A window would be nice right here, looking out on the garden."

"I can do that, if our friends here agree," said Cletus. Turning to The Peep and Kitten he added, "Tooth here is a marvelous cook."

"Really? We sure could use a good meal," said Kitten. "Been eating out of these jars for a few days now. The labels have worn off of most of them, so we're not always sure what we're getting. Strictly pot luck, you know."

"Well now, I saw some sprouts and herbs in the garden that will do nicely," said Tooth. "Kitten, you and The Peep pull four ears of that sweet corn. I think we'll need about five handfuls of those spring peas, too. Cletus and I will dig the root vegetables."

"Will there be cheese?" Cletus asked.

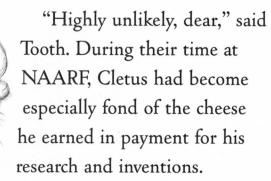

"Highly unlikely, dear," said Tooth. During their time at NAARF, Cletus had become especially fond of the cheese he earned in payment for his research and inventions.

That night the new friends dined on Tooth's Spring Chowder and Roasted Rutabagas. A day or so later Cletus finished work on a shop. In back he cleared a sleeping space for himself. Next he created a proper kitchen and a bedroom for Tooth. When all was complete, Tooth brought out her most prized possessions: quilts made long ago by Grandma Nellie—one for each bed.

"There now. A proper home that's safe from weasels," said Tooth.

"You bet," said Cletus.

Kitten Takes Off

Tooth and Cletus had settled right in. At mealtimes Tooth always concocted some lip-licking new dish. Together Cletus and Kitten had added wheels and a biodiesel engine to the Reed Basket.

One morning The Peep woke up early. He hopped out of the nesting box and looked over the edge of the loft. Kitten was not in his usual spot.

"Peep, peep, peep!" he called. No answer. The Peep tumbled quickly down the stack of bales. He checked where Cletus had set up his workshop. No Kitten. The Peep looked all around

Tooth's kitchen. No Kitten there, either.

Out behind the barn, The Peep saw something swishing. Up and down. Back and forth. A furry black tail!

"Peep. *Peeeep!*" Kitten got a scolding.

"Hey, cool your jets, dude," Kitten whispered. "Be real quiet and I'll show you my secret stuff. But you can't tell *anybody*." The Peep got quiet. Kitten took out a box printed with fancy gold letters. He flipped the top open. "I got these from one of the weasels down at the riverbank. Look, they're real cigars!"

"Peep, peep, peep," said The Peep with great admiration.

"I got these matches, too," Kitten said. "Tonight when everybody's asleep, I'm gonna smoke me a cigar."

Just then Tooth appeared. "Oh, I think

not, sir!" she said. "What in the world were you thinking? Keeping company with those gongoozling weasels, indeed!" Tooth snatched up the offending box and went off muttering. "Cigars! Foul, fumiferous foolishness . . ."

Furious as he was to be parted from his secret stash, Kitten waited until Tooth was out of earshot.

"What does she know? She's not the boss of me!" He jumped into the Reed Basket and roared off down the road, leaving The Peep

alone in a cloud of dust. The Peep ran after Kitten, but could not keep up. Soon his friend was completely out of sight.

"Peep . . . peeeep," lamented The Peep as he slowly waddled back home.

All afternoon The Peep peered through the upper loft window waiting for Kitten. The sun went down, and still Kitten had not come back. Tooth laid out a nice plate of doodlebug burgers, but The Peep refused to eat. What if Kitten never came back? The Peep started to cry. Little bubbles came out of the holes on either side of his bill.

"Oh now, little one, don't worry! I'm sure Kitten will be back before you know it," said Tooth.

That night The Peep just could not sleep. He paced around the edge of the nesting box, blowing those little bubbles. "Peep . . . peeep," he blubbered. With all the pacing and blubbering, Tooth and Cletus couldn't sleep, either. Tooth climbed up into the loft and pulled out Kitten's blanket. She called down to Cletus, "Maybe a bit of this will help!"

"Yes, of course, a transitional object. Could be just the ticket."

Using a piece of the soft, old blanket, Tooth made a cape for The Peep. It didn't help much. The Peep moped back and forth. He cried and sniffled, producing still more bubbles. After a long while, The Peep stopped and lay down.

"Whew!" said Cletus.

"Yes, indeed!" said Tooth. The

two mice tiptoed to their beds.

The next morning Tooth and Cletus discovered The Peep doing daredevil leaps off the side of the loft, just the way Kitten often did. The Peep flapped frantically as he plummeted down the stack of hay bales.

"Dear me," said Tooth, "this is serious!"

"Time for a poultice?" asked Cletus.

"*Hmm*. I'll see what I have on hand. You'd better go and find Kitten. That'll be our best remedy, I think."

"Without a doubt. I can do that," Cletus said.

Tooth ushered The Peep into the kitchen. She turned to her neatly organized assortment of bottles and jars. "*Hmm* . . . what have we got for a lonely heart?" She rummaged and sorted.

Tooth turned her back and The Peep looked up into the cabinet. There was Kitten's box of cigars where Tooth had tucked them away. When Tooth turned around again, The Peep was gone.

The Peep hopped right up to the loft, opened the forbidden box, took out the secret items, and lit up a long, brown cigar. Just then the Kitten drove the Reed Basket into the barn.

"Gotta get my blanket, then I'm gone. Can't stay where no one understands what I'm about," he grumbled. But his blanket was not where he had left it. Then Kitten saw The Peep. He was standing in a cloud of stinky smoke.

"Pip, *pipp!*" coughed The Peep.

"Man, you don't look too good," said Kitten. He spied the cigar box. "Hey, give that here!"

But he didn't have time to finish. The Peep, overjoyed, had stretched his wings wide to give

his friend a hug. The cigar fell. Flames shot up
from the straw-covered floor, spreading in every
direction. Kitten and The Peep ran to the far
corner of the loft.

"Hey, Fire! Fire! H-HELP!" cried Kitten.

"PEEP! PEEP! PEEP!" shouted The Peep.

Tooth came running. She raced up the
burning hay bales, determined to save the
young ones. "This way,
quickly!" she cried.
But it was too late.
Both cat and duckling
were trapped behind the
flames. The smoke rose
up in great clouds. Tooth
could no longer see Kitten
or The Peep. "Oh, mercy!"
she cried.

Suddenly it began to rain inside the barn. A big, whizzling rain. It showered down on the fire, and on Kitten, The Peep, and Tooth. The flames died down. The soaking waterfall kept going.

"Oh, jolly good! I see it's working," Cletus said, as he strolled back into the barn. "New sprinkler system. Heat activated. Thought it might come in handy with all this dry tinder about." Turning to Kitten he said, "I see you've made it back in time for dinner, my friend."

"So that's what you've been working on late at night!" said Tooth. "Cletus, you are the maestro of moisture. I've always said you're a wonder. This invention certainly proves the point!"

Cletus said, "Thank you, my dear." He sniffed. "Phew! It stinks of cigar in here. Who would be smoking one of those nasty things in a barn full of hay?"

"Not me," said Kitten, "not ever!" He held up a soggy shape. "Look, here's a whole box of 'em, all soaked and ruined."

"And good riddance, I say!" piped Tooth.

"Peep . . . peep!" said The Peep.

"Yeah," said Kitten.

"Well I'm glad that's settled. Let's get you two cleaned up. You're both sodden with wet soot from head to foot," said Tooth.

Kitten put his arm around The Peep. "Man, you gotta be careful. You may be waterproof, but you're definitely not fireproof."

"Peep, peep, peep," said The Peep.

No one said it, but everyone in the barn thought, *Yes. That's it exactly.*

Glossary

biodiesel [BY-oh-dee-zul]—An engine that runs on vegetable oil

concocted [kon-KOKT-ed]—To prepare by mixing, or to devise

fumiferous [fyoom-IF-er-us]—Smokey

gongoozling [gon-GOOZ-ling]—Staring for hours at anything out of the ordinary

hillocks [HIL-uks]—Small hills

maestro [MY-stroh]—An artist of great skill

nefarious [ni-FARE-ee-us]—Extremely wicked

ominous [AHM-uh-nus]—Threatening

penthouse [PENT-hous]—An apartment located on

the top floor of a building

poultice [POLE-tus]—Medicine consisting of a soft
heated mass of meal or clay that is spread on a
cloth and applied to the skin

riddance [RID-uns]—The act of removing or getting
rid of something

scalawag [SKAL-uh-wag]—A deceitful and
unreliable person

serendipitous [ser-un-DIP-it-us]—Lucky or
fortunate

sodden [SOD-un]—Wet through and through

tinder [TIN-der]—Dry material that easily catches
fire from a spark

titanium [tie-TANE-ee-um]—A light, strong,
lustrous, corrosion-resistant metal

transitional object [tran-ZI-shun-ul OB-jekt]—An
item that serves a soothing function for
children

About the Author

Amanda Lorenzo was born on the West Coast of the United States and has managed to live close to salt water ever since. She shares her home in Seattle, Washington, with her cool cat, Chiti. Amanda loves to sing and has taught music to children ages 5 to 13. She is often surprised by the funny and goofy things that her characters insist on doing, and finds herself laughing even when she knows how the story's going to end.

To invite Amanda Lorenzo to speak to your school or group, please visit www.RuntFarm.com.

About the Illustrator

Mark Evan Walker lives in the wilds of suburban Texas, and draws Runt Farm amidst mighty oaks, magnolias, and brilliantly colored crepe myrtle and althaeas. Mark would like to thank all the Runt Farmers for being so kind as to pose on those occasions when needed to help tell their stories. He would also like to thank Cletus for the suggestion about fixing his drawing board, and Tooth for the delicious blueberry pie. Yum!

Read a Sneak Preview of Runt Farm: Book 2!

Beatrice and Blossom

"Hey, I'm getting smushed here!" said the smallest bunny on the market truck. She pushed back against a rabbit she didn't recognize.

"What's that?" the older rabbit taunted. "Ha-ha-ha! Did anybody hear a *mouse*?"

A fidgety one joined in. "What's a matter, little *bay*-bee? Can't see over your own ears?"

"Listen, I'm getting mashed," she insisted. "Move over."

"We can't help it if you're a pipsqueak,

Beatrice," said a bigger bunny. "We grew so big that we are going to market, right guys?"

"*Right!*" shouted the group gleefully.

"You're so small no one will even be able to see you," added the big bunny, shoving Beatrice aside.

Beatrice shoved back. "Hey, get off me, you big hare!"

The fidgety one smoothed her whiskers. "Yes, we're definitely going to market. We don't even know why you were picked to come with us. You're a puny little *hare*ball. My baby brother's bigger than you are!"

Beatrice worked her paw into a fist and stuck it in Fidgety's face. "I'm big enough to punch the twitch outta your nose, fuzzhead!"

"Look, she is *so* small I bet she can't even stay in the hutch," said the big rabbit, giving

Beatrice a push. Sure enough, Beatrice popped out of the cage.

"Will you look at that!" cried the fidgety rabbit, clapping her paws to her muzzle. "What a baby! Ha-ha-ha!"

"Baby Bea, Baby Bea, look at her, she's only three!" taunted the group.

Beatrice whirled around to face the bunch in the cage. "I can *too* go to market!" she shouted. "I can if I want to!"

Suddenly the truck lurched around a corner, and Beatrice went rolling one way and then the other. She scrambled to her feet just inches away from the back of the truck and looked down. The road whizzing by so close to her feet made her feel dizzy.

To Ruthie

who told me many endearing stories

and listened to mine.

BooKTi
MooKTi
P R E S S

Published by BooktiMookti Press · Seattle, WA · www.booktimookti.com · FIRST EDITION · Book Design by Shannon McCafferty · Library of Congress Cataloging-in-Publication Data · Lorenzo, Amanda · Under New Management / by Amanda Lorenzo · Illustrations by Mark Evan Walker · Summary: A group of small animals make a home on an abandoned farm. 1. Animals—Fiction 2. Family—Fiction · I. Walker, Mark Evan ill II. Title III. Series Lorenzo, Amanda Runt Farm Series bk 1 · ISBN 13: 978-0-9800952-0-3

visit www.RuntFarm.com

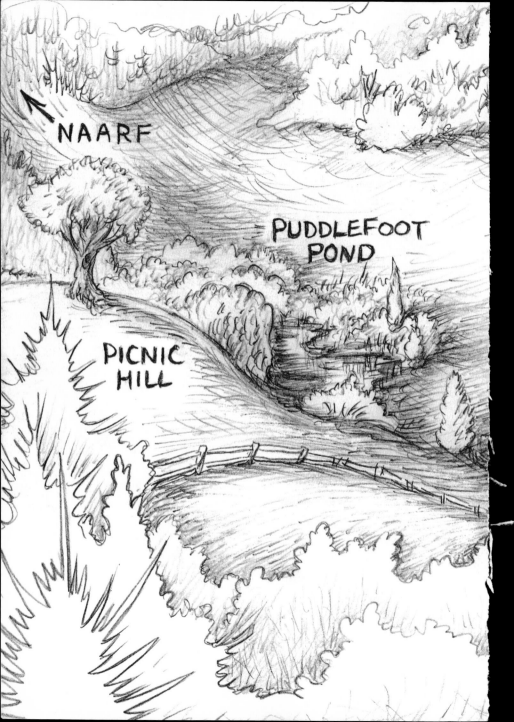